S.R. Calthrop

A Lecture on Physical Development, and its Relations to Mental and Spiritual Development

SALZWASSER
VERLAG

S.R. Calthrop

A Lecture on Physical Development, and its Relations to Mental and Spiritual Development

Reprint of the original, first published in 1859.

1st Edition 2022 | ISBN: 978-3-37512-290-4

Verlag (Publisher): Salzwasser Verlag GmbH, Zeilweg 44, 60439 Frankfurt, Deutschland
Vertretungsberechtigt (Authorized to represent): E. Roepke, Zeilweg 44, 60439 Frankfurt, Deutschland
Druck (Print): Books on Demand GmbH, In de Tarpen 42, 22848 Norderstedt, Deutschland

A

LECTURE

ON

PHYSICAL DEVELOPMENT, AND ITS RELATIONS TO MENTAL AND SPIRITUAL DEVELOPMENT,

DELIVERED BEFORE THE

AMERICAN INSTITUTE OF INSTRUCTION,

AT THEIR

TWENTY-NINTH ANNUAL MEETING,

IN

NORWICH, CONN., AUGUST 20, 1858.

BY

S. R. CALTHROP,

OF BRIDGEPORT, CONN.,

FORMERLY OF TRINITY COLLEGE, CAMBRIDGE, ENGLAND.

BOSTON:

TICKNOR AND FIELDS.

M DCCC LIX.

On motion of G. F. THAYER, — *Voted*, unanimously, That five thousand copies of MR. CALTHROP's Lecture be printed at the expense of the Institute, for gratuitous circulation.

LECTURE.

MR. PRESIDENT, LADIES AND GENTLEMEN : —

WE have met together to consider the best
methods of Educating, that is, drawing out, or
developing the Human Nature common to all of
us. Truly a subject not easy to be exhausted.
For we all of us feel that the Human Nature, —
out of whose bosom has flowed all history, all
science, all poetry, all art, all life in short, — con-
tains within itself far more than that which has
hitherto been manifested through all the periods of
its history, though that history dates from the crea-
tion of the world, and has already progressed as far
as the nineteenth century of the Christian era. Yes!
we all of us feel that the land of promise lies far
away in the future, that the goal of human history
is yet a long way off.

A large portion of this assembly consists of those
whose business it is to study Human Nature in all
its various forms, and who have taken upon them-

selves the task of developing that nature in the youth of America, in that rising generation whose duty it will be to carry out the nascent projects of reform in every department of human interest, and make the thought of to-day the fact of to-morrow.

Some doubtless there are among this number, who by very nature are born Teachers, called to this office, as by a voice from heaven! Men, who in spite of foolish detraction, or yet more foolish patronage, understand the dignity, the true nobility of their calling; who know that the office of the teacher is coëval with the world; and also feel with true prophetic foresight, that the world, fifty years hence, will be very much what its Teachers intend, by God's blessing, to make it.

Brothers in a high calling! The speaker, proudly enrolling himself in the number of your noble band, greets you from his heart this day, and invites you to spend a thoughtful hour with him; and to help him, by your best wishes, to unfold in a manner not wholly unworthy of his theme, some small portion of the nature and method of Human Development.

Ours is the age of analysis. We begin to see that before we can understand a substance, it is necessary to become acquainted with all its component parts. Thus, then, with regard to Human Nature, we must understand all at least of its grand divisions, before we can comprehend the method of developing it as a whole.

Let us then say, that there are five grand divisions

in Human Nature, — the physical, the intellectual, the affectional, the moral, and the devotional, — or in other words, that man has body, mind, heart, conscience, and soul.

Concerning these great divisions, I shall assert, *first*, that they are all mutually dependent upon each other; that if one of them suffer, all the others suffer with it; that man is dwarfed and incomplete, unless he is fully developed in all the five: and, *secondly*, as my special subject, I maintain that physical well-being, health of body, is therefore necessary not only to the complete development of Human Nature, but that it is also essential to a happy and harmonious development of each one of the four other great divisions of Human Nature; or in other words, I assert the body has something to do both with the mind, heart, conscience, and soul of man, not merely to all these collectively, but also to each of them separately.

First, then, I shall speak on the mutual dependence of the faculties.

Now, although it is not possible that any faculty should be so completely isolated, as to act without moving any of the rest at all; nevertheless, since a comparative isolation and separation of the faculties is but too common, let us glance through the history of the past, and mark any notable instances of such isolation; and if we find that a one-sided development has always proved a failure, we shall begin to discern the folly of trying such disastrous experiments over again, specially since they would have to be made upon living human beings, upon

1*

the young children of the rising generation, who cannot resent our folly, but whose distorted natures will be living proofs of our incapacity, of our impotence as educators, when the experiment tried for the thousand and first time fails yet again, as it always has done, and always will do to the world's end, while Human Nature remains the same.

Let us then take a few examples, which are not intended to stand the test of severe criticism, but which are only used as illustrations of the idea which we are now considering.

Let us then first suppose that the devotional element in man acts alone. The experiment has already been tried. Many a hermit in lonely cell or rocky cavern, has cut himself off from the society of men, from action, duty and love, in order that he may be devout without hindrance. How many such men have poured out their souls upon the ground, on barren sand or desert rock, souls which might have watered thousands with the dew of heaven, and all because they made one fatal life-mistake,—they thought, that to pray always meant to be always saying prayers.

Who could be more devout than Saint Simeon Stylites? who spent all his life upon the top of a tall pillar, absorbed in contemplation, ecstasy, remorse and prayer. Let the poet speak for him.

" Bethink thee, Lord? while Thou and all the saints
  Enjoy themselves in heaven, and men on earth
  House in the shade of comfortable roofs,
  Sit with their wives by fires, eat wholesome food
  And wear warm clothes, and even beasts have stalls,

I, 'twixt the spring and downfal of the light
Bow down one thousand and two hundred times
To Christ, the Virgin Mother and the Saints :
Or in the night, after a little sleep,
I wake, the chill stars sparkle ; I am wet
With drenching dews, or stiff with crackling frost,
I wear an undressed goatskin on my neck,
And in my weak, lean arms I lift the Cross,
And strive and wrestle with Thee till I die.
O mercy, mercy, wash away my sin ! ".

A mournful spectacle. Devotion excited to madness, while mind, heart, and conscience, all are dumb, and the poor weak body only bears the heavy burdens which the tyrannous soul heaps upon it!

Devotion, then, needs *conscience*. Conscience tells a man that he must act as well as pray. Devotion makes the great act of prayer. Conscience works out into the actual of every-day life, the ideal of which devotion has conceived. Will then devotion and conscience be sufficient for a noble manhood? Devotion and conscience alone developed, have oft-times, in the days that are past, formed some stern old grand inquisitor, torturing the life out of human sinews because he ought. The grand inquisitor's devotion and conscience told him that he ought to advance the holy faith by every engine in his power, and therefore, as he considered that the rack, the thumbscrews, the rope, the fire and the faggot were the best possible engines, he used the same to the utmost of his ability; and thought, alas for humanity! that he was doing God service.

The grand inquisitor had devotion, he had conscience, he probably also had nerves of iron; but he could not possibly have had a *heart.* Devotion, then, and conscience need a loving, human heart. Will these three be sufficient? The picture grows fairer, we begin to feel less pain when we turn away from the stern, dark portrait of the grand inquisitor, which frowns so grimly in the picture gallery of history, and look upon that fair and gentle upturned face, half shaded by the veil that covers her head. That is a nun of the order of Saint Theresa.

The pale, emaciated countenance tells of many a vigil protracted through the long hours of the night; those wild eyes once saw, or thought they saw, the picture of the Virgin hanging in her cell smiling on her as she prayed; yea, and have wept many a tear as she repeated her sins over to her confessor, or as she stood by the bed-side of some poor sufferer, while those gentle Christian hands smoothed the dying pillow. Rest in peace, soul sainted and dear! The tears thou didst once shed, are wiped away now forever; the sins thou didst once bewail, are all forgiven now, for thou hast loved much!

But the day of nuns has gone forever. A higher development must be sought for. The nun becomes impossible when we train the *intellect;* Devotion says, Worship; the Mind adds, The Lord thy God. The Conscience says, Do right; the Intellect shows what is right. The Heart says, Love thy fellow-men; the Intellect tells the right way of loving them. Piety and charity! these arc glorious! these are the two angels from Heaven which prompt us to help our brothers who need our help; but intellect must show us the way to do it. To take a single instance. Piety and charity cannot show us how to drain and ventilate and rebuild the hovels of the poor in New York. No, every spade, every saw, every hammer employed in that most righteous undertaking must be directed by intellect, by science. Piety and charity may prompt, but intellect must guide.

I know full well that many a woman's heart, guided only by her sacred instinct of loving, acts out the law of right without any conscious questioning of the intellect; that a thousand tender feet carry the gospel of Christ along the alleys of New York and London, or along the corridors of the Crimean hospital, though even there also woman's wit has to aid woman's heart. The noble heart, the Christian love of Florence Nightingale took her to those eastern shores; this made the voice tender and the hand gentle. But whoso reads the account of what she did, will see that beside these, wit and wisdom, keen discerning of means to ends, ability to see what ought to be done, intellect, reason in short, was necessary in order to make a Florence Nightingale possible, together with an exhaustless fund of bodily endurance, fortitude and stoicism.

Thus, then, we find that devotion, conscience, heart, and intellect are all necessary to each other in the harmonious development of Human Nature. Will they be found sufficient for a perfect life?

Put together a strong soul, a tender conscience, a woman's heart, and a man's intellect, and we have a Charlotte Brontë, — surely one of the best types of the modern mind. Will she find these four noble parts of Human Nature sufficient for the task of living?

Let Charlotte Brontë answer, walking painfully across the moor with hand held hard to beating side, sitting now and then upon a stone to keep herself from falling, wondering why the daylight blinds her so, obliged to give up Villette owing to the terrible headaches which it brings on. Let Charlotte Brontë answer, dying before her time at thirty-nine years of age, when the path of fame was just beginning to be bright before her, and the world was just beginning to know how much it wanted her. Charlotte Brontë, the gifted and the feeble, the lynx-eyed and the blind, so full of glorious strength and pitiable weakness! Charlotte Brontë, who feels the pressure of every-day life to be as hard as a giant's grasp upon her throat! Charlotte Brontë cannot tell why she is so unhappy, why she feels like a prisoner in the world, — why earth, our beautiful earth, is like a charnel house to her. And yet we think that the most ordinary passer by could see very satisfactory reasons why Charlotte Brontë was what she was, and felt what she felt. Hollow cheek and faded eye, teach their wisdom to their possessor last of all. The pale-eyed school-girl, who never played along with the other children, never ran and laughed and shouted with the rest, little knew what days and hours and years of dulness, of pain and agony, she was laying up for the future, what a premature grave she was digging for herself. Peace be with her, her toil is over; it is now three years since Heaven received in Charlotte Brontè one angel more.

Intellect, then, needs *body*. Come, then, and see me build a Man! A calm, silent devotion, a conscience pure and reverent, a heart manful and true, an intellect clear and keen, a frame of iron,—with these will we dower our hero, and call him Washington!

From me Washington needs no eulogy. Free America is at once his eulogy and his monument! It is useless to say more. Every one here feels in his heart a higher praise than can be uttered by the tongue. But let me ask you, What would Washington's qualities of mind and heart have availed his country, unless the manly strength, the frame of iron had been added? A good man he might have been, a patriot he surely would have been; but the Father of his Country, never! The soul that trusted in God, the conscience that felt the omnipotence of justice and right, the heart that beat for his country's weal alone, the mind that thought out her freedom, was upborne by the body that knew no fatigue, by the nerves that knew not how to tremble.

Washington had to endure physical fatigue enough to have killed three ordinary men. And how well did his youth prepare him for a life of protracted toil. Hear his biographer Irving. " He was a self-disciplinarian in physical as well as mental matters, and practised himself in all kinds of athletic exercises, such as running, leaping, pitching quoits, and tossing bars. His frame even in infancy had been large and powerful, and he now excelled most of his playmates in contests of agility and strength. As a proof of his muscular power, a place is still pointed out at Fredericksburg, near the lower ferry, where, when a boy, he threw a stone across the river. In horsemanship, too, he already excelled, and was ready to back, and able to manage, the most fiery steed. Traditional anecdotes still remain of his achievements in this respect."

Some of you have doubtless seen in Thackeray's 'Virginians,' that young Warrington found that he was more than a match for the English jumpers, as indeed, writes he, he ought to be, as he could jump twenty-one feet and a half, and no one in Virginia could beat him, except Colonel G. Washington.

It is needless to say that I do not mean to exalt the body at the expense of the higher faculties. I only maintain that the rest are incomplete without the physical element; in which indeed all the other powers dwell, and by means of which they are more or less clearly manifested. There may, of course, be vast physical energy without any corresponding development of mind or soul, as any blacksmith or prize fighter could tell us. And further, there may be a character, in which some of the higher qualities may exist in great perfection, coupled, too, with mighty force of body, and yet the character may be

incomplete.   Take, as an instance, another of
America's great men.

Daniel Webster! perhaps the most cavernous
head, set upon the strongest shoulders, which has
appeared upon the planet, since the soul of Socrates
went back to God.   Daniel Webster! strong mind
in strong body, leader and king of men, deep-chested,
lion-voiced, whose words of power moved men as
the wind moves the sea, whose eloquence had a
physical energy, a bodily grandeur about it like to
that of no other man.   Daniel Webster! pride of all
Americans; to you I leave it to say where he was
weak.   It belongs not to me, a stranger, to pluck
one laurel from that stately brow; his own brethren
must do it, with reluctant and half remorseful hands,
pitying the errors which marred so grand a character, but saying of him as I would say of England,
Webster, with all thy faults, I love thee still.

Our analysis of human character, necessarily one-
sided and imperfect, is now ended.   It remains for
us to ask, What are its bearings upon American
education?   How far does American education
fulfil the wants of Human Nature, and wherein does
it disregard them?   The title of my Lecture tells
plainly enough, where I think that the great
deficiency is found; a deficiency which reacts
upon both mind and morals, and ofttimes utterly
defeats the best efforts of clergymen and teachers.
I assert, then, that, in America, the body is almost
entirely neglected.   Thirty thousand clergymen,
from as many pulpits, advocate the claims of the
conscience and the soul.   A hundred thousand

teachers are busied throughout the length and breadth of the land in training the intellect, while a man could almost count on his fingers the number of those engaged in training the body. The intellectual training which the masses receive, is the highest glory of American education. If I wanted a stranger to believe that the Millennium was not far off, I would take him to some of those grand Ward Schools in New York, where able heads are trained by the thousand. When I myself entered them, I was literally astonished. When I looked at the teachers who instructed that throng of young souls, I could not help saying to myself, Ah! dear friends, it would do you good to know what I feel just now. I can feel the very blessing of God descending on your labors, just as if I could see it with mine eyes. What piety have been at work here, in the construction of this colossal system of education! What inspired energy was needed to work it out! What charity is necessary to carry it on! Many a teacher saw I there, unknown, may-be, to all the world, carrying on her work with noble zeal and earnestness, to whom the quick young brains around bore abundant testimony. When I saw them, I blessed them in my heart, I magnified mine office, and said to myself, I, too, am a teacher.

I spent four or five days doing little else than going through these truly wonderful schools. I stayed more than three hours in one of them, wondering at all I saw, admiring the stately order, the unbroken discipline of the whole arrangements, and the wonderful quickness and intelligence of the scholars. That same evening I went to see a friend, whose daughter, a child of thirteen, was at one of the ward schools. I examined her in algebra, and found that the little girl of thirteen could hold her own with many of a larger growth. Did she go to school to-day? asked I. No, was the answer, she has not been for some time, as she was beginning to get quite a serious curvature of the spine, so now she goes regularly to a gymnastic doctor.

I almost feel ashamed to criticize such noble institutions as the schools of New York; but truth compels me to do this. Hitherto, nothing whatever has been done to train the bodies of the tens of thousands who are educated there. All that is done is excellent, is wonderful, but fearful drawbacks come into play, in the shape of physical weakness, and positive male-formation of body.

The only remedy which can be devised, I think, in a crowded city like New York, where it is impossible to get open ground, is to have large gymnasiums attached to every ward school, and daily exercise therein should form an essential part of the education there. The importance of this to New York cannot be estimated, and I heard with joy, that a gymnasium was established in at least one of the ward schools, and I found out that the teachers of others were alive to this most crying need. I read too, with very great pleasure, that a Mr. Sedgwick of New York was appointed to deliver a lecture on the importance of physical education, at the next meeting of the Teachers Association, in that State; and indeed every one begins to feel that

something must be done, and that quickly. Miss
Beecher's book enlightened most people on this
subject, and reform is already inaugurated. It is
well that it is so, or the race would dwindle away
before our very eyes. Listen to some serio-comic
verse upon this subject, taken out of your Lecturer's
portfolio. It is an address to America, dictated by
an ancient sage : —

> ' Oh ! latest born of time, the wise man said,
> A mighty destiny surrounds thy head ;
> Great is thy mission, but the puny son
> Lacks strength to finish what the sires begun ;
> Thy hapless daughters breathe the poison'd air,
> Fair they may be, but fragile more than fair ;
> They know not, doom'd ones, that the air of heaven,
> For breathing purposes to man was given ;
> They know not half the things which life requires,
> But melt their lives away where stoves and fires,
> And furnace issuing from the realms beneath,
> Distils through parlor floors its poisonous breath.
> Sooner or later must the slighted air
> And exercise take vengeance on the fair.
> Ah ! one by one I see them fade and fall,
> Both old and young, fair, dark or short or tall,
> Till one stupendous ruin wraps them all.'

One can sometimes, in a smiling way, give utterance
to truths which seem hard and stern when spoken
in grim earnest. Let us see whether we cannot
find some allegory to represent what we mean.

Some time ago, I read a tale which related that
a certain gentleman was, once on a time, digging
a deep hole in his garden. He had, as I myself had
in my younger days, a perfect passion for digging
holes, for the mere pleasure of doing it; but the

hole which he was now digging was by far the deepest which he had ever attempted. At last he became perfectly fascinated, carried away by his pursuit, and actually had his dinner let down to him by a bucket. Well, he dug on late and early, when just as he was plunging in his spade with great energy for a new dig, he penetrated right through, and fell down, down to the centre of the earth.

To his astonishment he landed upon the top of a coach which was passing at the time, and soon found himself perfectly at home, and began to enter into conversation with the passenger opposite to him, a very gentlemanly looking man enveloped entirely in a black cloak. He soon found out that the country into which his lot had fallen was a very strange one. Its peculiarities were thus stated by his gentlemanly fellow-passenger. "Ours, Sir," said he, "is called the country of Skitzland. All the Skitzlanders are born with all their limbs and features perfect; but when they arrive at a certain age, all their limbs and features which have not been used drop off, leaving only the bones behind. It is rather dark this evening, or you would have seen this more plainly. Look forward there at our coachman, he consists simply of a stomach and hands, these being the only things he has ever used. Those two whom you see chatting together are brothers in misfortune; one is a clergyman, the other a lawyer; they have neither of them got any legs at all, though each of them possess a finely developed understanding; and you cannot help remarking what a massive

2*

jaw the lawyer has got. Yonder is Mr. ————, the celebrated millionaire, he is just raising his hat; you see he has lost all the top part of his head, indeed he has little of his head left, except the bump of acquisitiveness and the faculty of arithmetical calculation. There are two ladies, members of the fashionable world, their case is very pitiable, they consist of nothing whatever but a pair of eyes and a bundle of nerves. There are two members of the mercantile world, they are munching some sandwiches, you see, but it is merely for the sake of keeping up appearances; as I can assure you, from my own personal knowledge, that they have no digestive organs whatever. As for myself, I am a schoolmaster. I have been a hard student all my life, at school and at college, and moreover I have had a natural sympathy with my fellow-men, and so I am blessed with a brain and heart entire. But see here." And he lifted up his cloak, and lo! underneath, a skeleton, save just here! "See, here are the limbs I never used, and therefore they have deserted me. All the solace I now have consists in teaching the young children to avoid a similar doom. I sometimes show them what I have shown you. I labor hard to convince them that most assuredly the same misfortune will befall them which has happened to me and to all the grown-up inhabitants; but even then, I grieve to say, I cannot always succeed. Many believe that they will be lucky enough to escape, and some of the grown-up inhabitants pad themselves, and so cheat the poor children into the belief that they are all right, though all the elder ones know better. You will now perceive the reason why all the gentlemen you see wear such tight pantaloons, they pretend that it is fashionable, but in reality it is in order to prevent their false legs from tumbling out. Surely my case is miserable enough; my only hope consists in the idea of educating the rising generation to do better. No doubt it is easy to persuade them to do so in the country from which you come, but I assure you," added he with a heartfelt sigh, "that it is sometimes very hard to do so here. Nearly all of us, then, have lost something of our bodies. Some have no head, some no legs, some no heart, and so on; the less a man has lost, the higher he ranks in the social scale; and our Aristocracy, the governing body, consists of the few individuals who have used all their faculties, and therefore now possess them all."

At this moment a dreadful earthquake broke out, and an extempore volcano shot the gentleman who had listened to this interesting narration right up to the crust of the earth again, and by a strange and fortunate chance shot him up into the very hole which he had been digging, and he discovered himself lying down at the bottom of the hole, feeling just as if he had awakened from a dream; and to his surprise, heard distinctly the voice of his wife crying out from the top, " Come, come, dear, you're very late, and supper is getting quite cold!"

The name of the country of Skitzland translated

into the vulgar tongue is the planet earth, and America is one of the portions thereof. If we were to look round in a circuit of a hundred miles, how many of the Skitzland aristocracy should we find, think you? What a dropping off of limbs and features there would be, if the letter of the law of Skitzland were carried out! But it is absolutely certain that this is in effect the law of nature, which does not act, it is true, all in a moment; but which slowly and truly tends to this. The Hindoo ties up an arm, for years together, as a penance, thinking thereby he does Brahma service; the limb with fatal sureness withers away, and rots. The prisoner in solitary confinement has his mind and faculties bound, fettered and tied, and by a law as fixed as that which keeps the stars in their places, the said prisoner's mind grows weaker, feebler, less sane, day by day. School children are confined six long hours in a close school-room, sitting in one unvarying posture, their lungs breathing corrupted air, no single limb moving as it ought to move, not the faintest shadow of attention being paid to heart, lungs, digestive organs, legs or arms, all these being bound down, and tied as it were; and so, by the stern edict of heaven, which, when man was placed upon earth, decreed that the faculties un-used should weaken and fail, we see around us thousands of unhealthy children whose brains are developed at the expense of their bodies; the ulti-mate consequence of which will be, deterioration of brain as well as body.

What is the remedy for all this? I have before

stated that in large crowded cities, gymnastic training, systematically pursued *as a study*, is the only
thing which seems possible to be done, and most
assuredly will be beneficial wherever it is intro-
duced. But there is a different method of physical
education, which can be pursued either exclusively,
or in association with gymnastics, which can be
followed up either in the country, or in towns,
where playgrounds can be obtained. This is the
method which I have invariably pursued myself,
namely, the systematic pursuit of health and
strength by all manner of manly sports and games.
I myself learnt to play and love these games at
school and at college. I have given them now
nearly four years' trial in my school, and every day
convinces me more and more of their beneficial
results.

I cannot tell how much physical weakness,
how much moral evil we have batted, and bowled,
and shinnied away from our door; but I do know
that we have batted and bowled away indolence,
and listlessness, and doing nothing, which I believe
is the Devil's greatest engine; and I also know
that the enthusiasm of the boys in these games
never dies out, their enjoyment never flags, for
these games supply the want of the boys' natures,
and keep their thoughts from straying to forbidden
ground.

Now these games are the very thing which that
portion of mankind called the sporting world,
have always loved and cherished. They have in-
fused the love of these games into the very bones

of Englishmen, and who knows how much good England owes to them! Let us then overlook for a while the religious world, the commercial world, the literary world, for they do not contain what we seek now, and let us look at this poor sister world, a world which seldom finds itself in such good company.

Each of these worlds has its work; the one we now have to do with, the sporting world, is a world probably as much decried, and with as much reason, as any. But see how pertinaciously this world will persist in coming up to the surface wherever a community of men may be. See how rigorously the Puritans tried to put down, or rather *squeeze* this heinous tendency out of Human Nature! But they did not succeed, though goodness knows, they tried hard enough. Yet it has come up again, and lo! it is now as vigorous as ever. Friends! I am finding fault with the Puritans in the very midst of their descendants. But what greater compliment could I pay these old Puritans than this? for their greatest glory is, that they left to their descendants the precious legacy of free thought! and so deeply imbedded is this in the very bones of the race, that they will gladly hear a stranger criticize and even condemn, a portion of the Puritan mind: knowing full well, that the fabric which they builded on the shores of this Continent is sufficient to bear witness to the real manhood that was in them. But what was the reason of their failure? Simply they were trying to drive out Nature with a pitchfork, and she of course will perpetually keep coming back. So we say of this world, the sporting world, so liable to abuse, and so unsparingly abused, what is true of all the worlds, and that is, that it would be well for mankind, if they were to bestow a little thought upon the demands of this, as well as of the other worlds; and not be content to ignore wholly a thing the value of which they do not undestand;— how the sporting world has witnessed, does witness, and will forever witness, for a fact in Human Nature, which no amount of pressure will ever squeeze out of Human Nature, and that is, the necessity which human beings feel for amusement, and for open air exercise, not exercise merely, but hearty, joyous, blood-stirring exercise, with a good amount of pleasant emulation in it.

This, then, is what cricket and boating, battledore and archery, shinney and skating, fishing, hunting, shooting, and baseball mean, namely, that there is a joyous spontaneity in human beings; and thus Nature, by means of the sporting world, by means of a great number of very imperfect, undignified, and sometimes quite disreputable mouthpieces, is perpetually striving to say something deserving of far nobler and clearer utterance; something which statesmen, lawgivers, preachers, and educators would do well to lay to heart. My children, she would say, are not intended to be made working machines; they have capacities for joy, for spontaneous action, for doing some pleasant thing for the mere sake of doing it, without any regard to gain or profit, whether it be of money or

anything else; and by obeying my dictates, they
will find riches which they never sought for, will
obtain gifts they never asked.

Why, a fast young man at an English Univer-
sity too often learns no good thing there, except to
play a capital game at cricket, have a good seat
upon a horse, pull an oar till he drops, and to have
a general belief in the omnipotence of pluck! And
I can tell you that is no bad education too, as far
as it goes. I am perfectly well aware that fast
young men too often learn other and worse things
than these, learn to drink, and swear, and debauch,
and to spend as fast as possible in riotous living
the manhood and strength which God has given
them. But this I know and publicly declare, that
it is this love of manly sports which keeps the fast
young men of England from utter corruption and
decay. Such men, renowned in their school and
college days as good cricketers, oarsmen or riders,
were the men that made Alma, Inkermann, and
Balaklava possible; who have just done battle at
fearful odds on the burning plains of India, on
behalf of helpless women and slaughtered babies;
and those whom their strong right arm could not
save, it was able to avenge! The iron endurance
which they had gained in many a bloodless contest,
stood them in good stead there, when all their
manhood was needed, if ever it was; and over
those that nobly died there, methinks that I can
see the Genius of England weep bitter tears, and
thus speak with deep self-reproach:—" Ah! sons
of mine! loved and early lost! ye whom I could

not teach, whom no one in all my broad lands could teach, how to unite the virtuous, wise and holy soul, together with the soul joyous and free! Alas! for me, that ye had to die, before I could know how noble ye were! that your cold bodies, fallen on the field, wounds all in front, and none behind, would be so many poor dumb mouths to tell me of the untold wealth which I have in my children, those very ones who too often are nought but shame and grief to me!" Dear, noble old England! if God will teach her this wisdom, her old heart will beat on bravely for a thousand years to come.

The preponderance of the animal, the bodily element, produces fast young men; and fast young men, and boys tending to become such, are the problem of society, the terror of the peace-loving, money-making world, and the scandal of the Educator, as he himself feels well enough his own impotence in dealing with them.

I have seen many an Educator who has felt that he ought to get at these young rebellious forces, but who does not know the way, and despairingly wonders why he cannot do so. Friend! I would say, no man can influence another, unless he has something akin to him. What do you think gives these blacklegs, men of not a tithe of your force and talent, such power over them? Why, it is community of nature, interests in common. But what interests have you in common with a fast young man? You know nothing that he knows, you admire nothing that he admires; and until you do really get a community of interest with him, you will be wide asunder as the poles, and the fast young man will remain, as he has hitherto remained, the one disgraceful problem which modern education cannot solve.

If an educator or college tutor wishes to influence this class of his scholars, or if a clergyman wishes to gain the souls of this part of his congregation, the one most difficult to deal with, let him join with them in some manly game, and let him assuredly know that whatever true manhood he has will stand him in good stead, and nothing else: nothing but real vital religion, real nobleness of character will be of any use in the cricket-field or the row-boat; and this will hold its own here as well as elsewhere.

Once, then, establish a community of interest on any one subject with young men, and you open to yourself a door, by which all good may enter. Nature, dear friends, makes nothing in vain, and it is of such infinite importance that strength of limb, readiness of eye and hand, physical vigor in short, should be transmitted from generation to generation, that she keeps producing fast young men, in spite of the thousand excesses which they commit, and will do so, until the ablest and wisest human minds take the matter in hand, and see to it that this part of Human Nature has its proper and legitimate food, guided by mind, thought, and reverence, instead of being allowed to run riot in all manner of wantonness.

The sporting world, then, with its manly games

and manly sports, gives us the means which are needed by the community at large for physical education; and the future educators of the country must be taught to love these manly games at school and at college, and then they will be able to disseminate them; whereas, at present, educators in this country are almost entirely ignorant of any manly games whatever. " But are not these games very dangerous," asks a careful mamma; " don't you find that boys get hurt very much by them? I have heard of some one who got his teeth knocked down his throat by them. Somebody else got his head hurt at shinney and so that was put a stop to, I believe, at Mr. ———'s school." Such mammas, doubtless, put into the hands of their children some good little book, with a narration of this sort. Little Johnny was told by his mamma not to climb trees. He was a good boy, and generally obedient. But one day he was in the garden of one of his schoolfellows, who asked him to climb a cherry tree; he forgot his mother's command, and went up, but after he had climbed nearly to the top his foot slipped, and down he tumbled through the branches on to the ground. He cried very much, and could not move, so they had to put him upon a shutter and carry him home. The doctor found that his leg was broken; the pain was dreadful when he had it set, &c. &c.; the drama ending by Johnny throwing his arms round his mother's neck, and declaring that if he ever got well, he would never disobey his dear, dear mother any more!

The good people who write these edifying stories

never seem to think whether it was wise for mamma
to forbid Johnny to climb a tree. Monkeys are
never forbidden to do so, and I seldom hear anything of their falling off. Poor people's children
climb trees, and there does not seem to be an
extraordinary increase of juvenile mortality on this
account. What should you say if some hard-
hearted person, myself for instance, were to say to
the dear mother of little Johnny, " Dear Madam,
you yourself, I grieve to say, were the cause of
Johnny's accident; you have habitually prevented
him from doing anything which would quicken his
perceptions and strengthen his limbs. He must
not soil his pinafore, he must not get his hands
dirty, and above all he must not play at any games
which make his hair untidy, or tear his clothes.
In fact, you have forbidden him to do precisely
those things which Nature prompted him to do.
He has generally been very obedient, you say, and
therefore his bodily powers have become weaker
instead of stronger. Well, the temptation came,
the unused and untrustworthy limbs were. sum-
moned to act, his consciousness of doing wrong
enfeebled him still further, and made them still more
nervous. He went up the tree, and the natural
consequence was, that he fell."

This, in substance, is the answer to all questions
of this class. I have played at cricket or shinney,
or boated, since I was nine years old. During the
last three years and a half, I have played at one or
the other almost every day. I have played at
shinney, or hockey, as we call it, all through the

winter, through snow a foot deep, and when the thermometer was below zero; I have played at cricket in summer with the thermometer at 90, and I have never yet seen one serious accident. The fact is, that I have a theory that Nature loves young men and boys, and love to aid them in their sports. She sends her ice and snow to educate them and make them hardy, while we are sitting by the stove and abusing the weather. She won't let them be hurt half as much by a blow or a fall, as older people who do not love her half as well. She breaks the young one's fall, and herself puts the plaster on his little fingers. She is delighted at every conquest that these young children of hers make over herself, just like some big boxer she stands, who is teaching his boy to box. He feints and threatens and looks big, but who so pleased as he when the young one gets in his one two!

Again, the danger is little or nothing to the daring and courageous. The fellow that isn't afraid of the ball, is scarcely ever hurt. He defends himself with eye and hand. The coward is the one most likely to get hurt. I think that there is just enough risk in these games to engender a manly contempt for pain, and a bold handling of a danger. If the cricket ball were a soft affair, it would be a game for babies not boys.

Let us then take a hint from the sporting world, and turn to the use of the many that which has formed the only redeeming feature of a few. The good that these manly games do, should not be confined to a small class, but should be diffused among the whole community, for the sporting world has something to say to all of us. It rouses the scholar from his desk, shakes him, and tells him that much study is a weariness to the flesh, and that the fields are alive with song. Out then he must come, and leave his musty books.

It comes to the business man in the crowded city, and babbles of green fields, nudges Mr. Sparrowgrass with its elbow, and tells him to take Mrs. S. and the children into the country.

It comes to Mr. Fezziwig at Christmas time, and tells him to let the young men in his shop have a jolly time of it, put by their work, listen to the fiddle, and join the dance.

Ay, and the dream of those half-forgotten days comes over Scrooge, the miserly, miserable Scrooge, and wakes up something like a soul in him.

It comes to Colonel Newcome, and bids him go to Charter House School, and take his boy out for a holiday.

This same spirit came to the ancient Greek in drama, dance and game, and with him was set to music, and consecrated to the gods, to Apollo the ever young, to Pallas the wise, to Bacchus the joy-giver.

It came to the stern old Roman with his Saturnalia, when for once in all the year the slave and the plebeian might speak their minds without fear.

It came to the dark-eyed Hebrew with his feasts of tabernacles, his feast of the harvest and the vintage, and over his joyaunce a sacred shadow rested, as of One who was over these things, who both made and consecrated the joy.

Spirit of joy! Wide as the world! Offspring of heaven! That descendest with airs redolent of thy native home, and comest to give to the toil-worn brickmakers of the earth a little rest! Forgive us, foolish dwellers in the clay, if ofttimes we take thy festal garlands, and drag them in the mire! drunk with the wine of thy pleasures, we turn thy gifts to ashes and to mourning. Come thou, nevertheless! and stay not, turn not away for our folly, come with thy love-light, and smile-light, and make the whole earth green with thy summer of delight.

It were a theme worthy of the place and time, if we could sketch out the progress of mankind; to show how God laid the foundations of the human race in the barbaric ages, strong, savage human bodies being the stones thereof; how in due order, order as sure and stately as that of the geologic eras, arose the Roman and the Greek, the types of full developed body and mind together: how in the fulness of time Christianity revealed the mighty powers of heart, conscience and soul, which before were lying dormant in the human race; so that now at last upon us has fallen the task of developing the whole of man,—body, mind, heart, conscience and soul.

But my time, if not your patience, fails me; so I leave it as a hint for future thought, and will in conclusion utter a few words of courage and hope for mankind, which each event of to-day seems to strengthen and enlarge. Yes, it is no longer fitting, that for the future we should have few hopers and many fearers. Nay, rather let us all join hands to-day, and form a great Electric Cable of Hope, that shall stretch from sea to sea, from shore to shore.

For it is certain, then, that the planet upon which God has placed us, is absolutely well fitted for the development of the human race. The more Science investigates, the more wonderful seems the adaptation of Human Nature to the world in which it is placed. The more refined a man becomes, the more delicate his insight into Nature, the more satisfied, the more overjoyed is he with her exhaustless charms. It is only our sin, our folly, our ignorance, which perpetually befools us, and robs us of our inheritance.

When the great coming race, prophesied of so long, shall at last inhabit the earth, they shall see no more glorious stars, no bluer atmosphere, than we do to-day; the moon shall pour forth no more silver from her bounteous horn; the sun shall lavish his golden rays no more freely, than he does to-day. But yet the whole world shall be unimaginably brighter and more beautiful to that crowning race. And why? Because their natures shall be in tune with the outward universe; their eyes and ears, and all their senses, shall be unimaginably more acute than ours; their bodies shall be perpetual sources of joy to them, and their souls shall be awake to knowledge, truth and love.

If our eyes were endowed with magnifying powers equal to that of some colossal telescope, how would the dome of heaven expand into inconceivable dimensions, the stars would be seen to be scattered along the sky like the sands upon the sea-shore. Each bright particular star would be magnified a thousand times, seeming vastly larger, and yet vastly more distant. The whole concave of heaven then would appear a thousand times larger than it does to our eyes, that is, it would appear a thousand times over ·more like its real size, though even then, eyes thus grandly gifted would fall immeasurably short of the reality of the universe which lies in the bosom of God! Now that great race of the future shall have their nature so in tune with things, and their spiritual conceptions so enlarged, that the great world shall be realized in its vastness, so much more vividly than we can conceive of it, that it shall be as if their material eye were exalted to the power of Lord Rosse's telescope.

Put together the fragments of men that we have amongst us to-day, — the physical joy in existence of the western hunter, the intellectual keenness of the man of science, the love of Nature of the artist or poet, the love for each little bird and insect of the naturalist, the justice of a Washington, the love for God and man of a Florence Nightingale, and then we gain some glimpses of the men of the future whom God has willed shall possess the planet at last. For assuredly the race is safe, though nations or individuals may fail and perish. Safe, because God has not built the planet in vain; safe, because his long patience shall have its full satisfaction at the last. How shall these things be? God will give this blessing to human labor directed by truth and love.

From partial and one-sided cultivation of Human Nature, partial and one-sided results can alone ensue. The commencement of this glorious era will date from the first complete education of all the manifold nature of man. The grand work once inaugurated, by the wondrous law of hereditary descent, natures completer and nobler on all sides will be the heritage of the next generation, by virtue of their birth, and so on in stately progression each generation shall expand and transmit a larger power to the generation that succeeds it; and at last the grand universe of matter shall put the world of man to shame no longer, but man with God's image shining through him, shall be seen to be worthy of the glorious nature in whose bosom he dwells.

See to it then, Educators! that young Human Nature has its due. See to it that conscience and the soul have their rightful supremacy, that intellect and sweet human affection walk hand in hand. And lastly, see to it, Educators! that these young bodies have their due. Learn for yourselves numberless manly sports and games, and resolutely continue to teach them and practise them yourselves in the midst of your scholars. Love open air and exercise yourselves first; this love will be contagious, and will communicate itself to those around you. No atom of true dignity will be lost, and a priceless fund of good humor will be gained for yourself, and a mutual good feeling will be established forever between you and your scholars. Do this, and we shall no longer hear of schoolmasters becoming old men before they are forty; but the schoolmaster will be known as the youngest looking, healthiest and happiest man in the district.

Upon us, my friends, more than upon any other class of men, this great, this lamentably neglected duty devolves. We are to see to it that young limbs and lungs have their rights; we must make men understand that it will be a sin against God, if they do not have their rights; a sin, whose punishment is as certain as the law of gravitation. And more, it must be our task to make men understand the inevitable blessing which is sure to descend upon the keeping of God's commandments written upon the body.

Schoolmaster in country village! whose two dollars per diem are begrudged and shaved down by some committee of boobies! whose lot, may-be, is additionally blessed by the privilege of boarding out among the exceedingly willing inhabitants of the district! upon thee no foolish word of pity shall fall from lips of mine! Thee no wise man will pity, but rather bid thee be of good cheer and play the man! Witness thou, in thy little corner of the great world, for all Human Nature. See thou that each part has its due, in the little flock of which thou art shepherd. Be faithful to thy sacred trust, and eyes yet unborn shall shine with the truth-light which thou didst first impart. Yea, generations shall rise up and call thee blessed!

By thee the young nerves, and limbs, and brain shall be loved, and pitied, and understood. Thou, like another Greatheart, shalt shield them from ignorance and wrong. To thee no word of man can matter much. Whether thou be praised or despised of men, is to thee a small thing; for in the calm eventide, when the day's work is over, thou hast ears to listen to the Master's voice, saying to his servant, Well done!